IF HE'S MY BROTHER

BY BARBARA WILLIAMS

ILLUSTRATED BY TOMIE DePAOLA

PRENTICE-HALL, INC.
ENGLEWOOD CLIFFS, N.J.

If He's My Brother
by Barbara Williams

Text copyright © 1976
by Barbara Williams

Illustrations copyright © 1976
by Tomie de Paola

Treehouse Paperback edition published 1980
by Prentice-Hall, Inc. by arrangement
with Harvey House, Publishers

Library of Congress Catalog Number 75-27480
Printed in the United States of America · J
ISBN 0-13-450627-8
10 9 8 7 6 5 4 3 2 1

ABOUT THE BOOK

What child has never asked the question, "If it's mine, why can't I do with it what I want?" This human characteristic is pursued in a whimsical vein by author Barbara Williams and artist Tomie de Paola, who have created a very funny picture book in which everyone can recognize something of himself. This perfect fusion of text and illustration will evoke chuckles from both children and adults. The simplicity and humor of the story will delight beginning readers.

FROM THE REVIEWS

"...for every child who has ever said... 'If it's mine, why can't I do what I want with it?' ...well served by de Paola's whimsical illustrations..."

—*Children's Book Review Service*

"...a series of questions that parents hear frequently... illustrated with de Paola's characteristically gentle humor, this will be enjoyed by children..."

—*School Library Journal*